*Once-Upon-A-Time*

# Three Tales of Three

*Goldilocks and the Three Bears*

*The Three Billy Goats Gruff*

*The Three Little Pigs*

Retold by Marilyn Helmer • Illustrated by Chris Jackson

*Kids Can Press*

*To Andrea, Marnie and all the librarians at Burlington Central
— thank you for your interest and encouragement. — M. H.*

*To Viv and Denise (Jackson) — two kids of three. — C. J.*

Text copyright © 2000 by Marilyn Helmer
Illustrations copyright © 2000 by Chris Jackson

All rights reserved. No part of this publication may be reproduced, stored in a retrieval system or transmitted, in any form or by any means, without the prior written permission of Kids Can Press Ltd. or, in case of photocopying or other reprographic copying, a license from CANCOPY (Canadian Copyright Licensing Agency), 1 Yonge Street, Suite 1900, Toronto, ON, M5E 1E5.

Kids Can Press acknowledges the support of the Ontario Arts Council, the Canada Council for the Arts and the Government of Canada, through the BPIDP, for our publishing activity.

Published in Canada by
Kids Can Press Ltd.
29 Birch Avenue
Toronto, ON  M4V 1E2

Published in the U.S. by
Kids Can Press Ltd.
4500 Witmer Estates
Niagara Falls, NY  14305-1386

The artwork in this book was rendered in ink and watercolor.
Text is set in Berkeley.

Series Editor: Debbie Rogosin
Editor: David MacDonald
Design: Marie Bartholomew
Printed in Hong Kong by Wing King Tong Company Ltd.

CM 00 0 9 8 7 6 5 4 3 2 1

**Canadian Cataloguing in Publication Data**

Helmer, Marilyn
    Three tales of three

(Once-upon-a-time)
ISBN 1-55074-759-2

1. Tales. 2. Fairy tales. I. Jackson, Chris, (date). II. Title. III. Series: Helmer, Marilyn. Once-upon-a-time.

PS8565.E459T47 2000    j398.2        C00-930010-4        PZ8.H3696Th 2000

Kids Can Press is a Nelvana company

# Goldilocks and the Three Bears

Long ago, in a neat little cottage in the forest, lived the Bear family. There was great big Papa Bear, middle-sized Mama Bear and teeny-weeny Baby Bear.

Every morning Papa Bear made a huge pot of oatmeal-raisin porridge. He put three heaping spoonfuls into his great big bowl, two heaping spoonfuls into Mama Bear's middle-sized bowl, and one heaping spoonful into Baby Bear's teeny-weeny bowl. Then the bears went for a walk in the forest while they waited for their porridge to cool.

One morning a little girl named Goldilocks went for a walk in the forest, too. As she skipped along, looking for someplace new to explore, she discovered a path she'd never noticed before. "I wonder where it leads," she said and, being a curious little girl, she decided to find out. So off she went, skipping and singing, until she came to a neat little cottage.

"What a pretty place," Goldilocks said to herself. She knocked on the door, but no one answered. She peeked in the keyhole, but no one was there.

Goldilocks pushed the door open, just a crack. Nothing happened. She pushed it a little further. Not a sound. "Should I or shouldn't I?" Goldilocks asked herself. Then, because *should* sounds better than *shouldn't*, she pushed the door all the way open and went inside.

On the table she found three bowls of oatmeal-raisin porridge. There was a great big bowl, a middle-sized bowl and a teeny-weeny bowl. Goldilocks was very hungry. "I'll just have a taste from each bowl," she promised herself.

She tried the porridge in the great big bowl. It was so hot it burned her tongue.

She tried the porridge in the middle-sized bowl. It was so cold it made her shiver.

She tried the porridge in the teeny-weeny bowl. "Just right," declared Goldilocks, and she ate every last bit.

Then Goldilocks peeked into the living room. She saw three chairs. There was a great big chair, a middle-sized chair and a teeny-weeny chair.

Goldilocks climbed onto the great big chair. "This one is much too hard," she said.

She bounced on the middle-sized chair. "This one's too soft," she said as she struggled out of it.

Then she plopped herself down in the teeny-weeny chair. "Just right," Goldilocks declared as she wiggled about on the seat. Suddenly, with a creak and a groan, the teeny-weeny chair broke into a dozen pieces. Goldilocks landed on the floor with a *whump!*

She scrambled to her feet and rubbed her bottom. Then she rushed off to explore the rest of the house.

In the bedroom Goldilocks found three beds — a great big bed, a middle-sized bed and a teeny-weeny bed.

She jumped onto the great big bed. "Too lumpy," she said.

She hopped onto the middle-sized bed. "Too bumpy."

Then she flopped down on the teeny-weeny bed. "Just right," declared Goldilocks, and she fell fast asleep.

When the three Bears returned from their walk, they were very hungry so they went right to the kitchen.

Papa Bear looked at his bowl. "Someone's been eating my porridge," he said in his great big voice.

Mama Bear looked at her bowl. "Someone's been eating my porridge, too," she said in her middle-sized voice.

Baby Bear held up his empty bowl. "Someone's been eating my porridge," he cried in his teeny-weeny voice. "And it's all gone!"

The three Bears went into the living room.

Papa Bear looked at his chair. The cushion was wrinkled. "Someone's been sitting in my chair," he said in his great big voice.

Mama Bear looked at her chair. The pillow was crinkled. "Someone's been sitting in my chair, too," she said in her middle-sized voice.

Baby Bear looked at his chair. There wasn't much there. "Someone's been sitting in my chair, and it's all broken to bits!" he wailed in his teeny-weeny voice.

"Someone has been in our house!" growled Mama Bear.

"I wonder who?" said Baby Bear.

The three Bears marched into the bedroom.

Papa Bear looked at his bed. The quilt was crumpled. "Someone's been sleeping in my bed," he said in his great big voice.

Mama Bear looked at her bed. The blanket was rumpled. "Someone's been sleeping in my bed, too," she said in her middle-sized voice.

Baby Bear looked at his bed. There lay Goldilocks, fast asleep. "I know who has been in our house," he squealed. "And she's still here!"

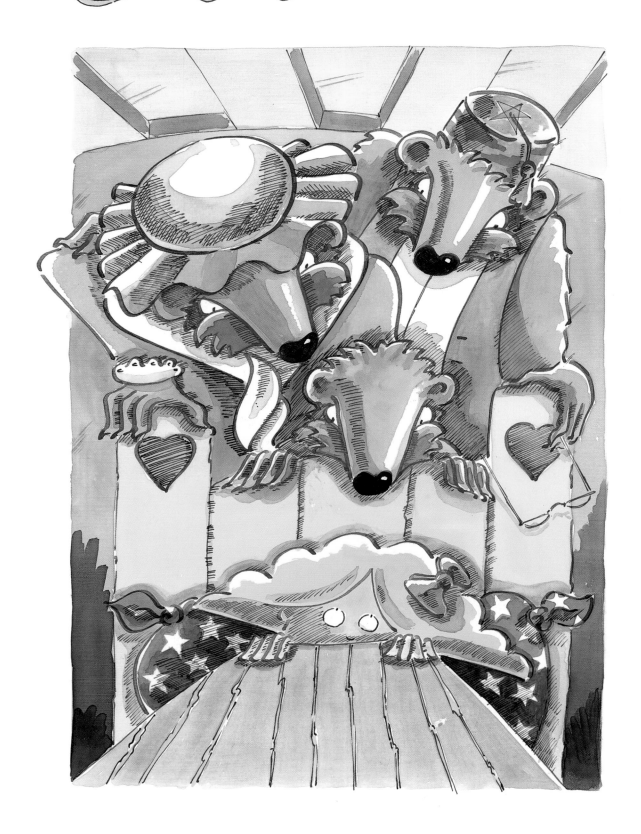

# The Three Billy Goats Gruff

Once upon a time there were three Billy Goat brothers whose name was Gruff.

One day they decided to graze high in the hills where there was plenty of clover, grass and wild berries to make them full and fat. To get to the hills, the Billy Goats Gruff had to cross a wobbly wooden bridge.

Under that bridge lived a wicked old Troll. He had eyes as red as burning coals and a long crooked nose that could sniff out anything for miles around.

The Troll claimed the bridge was his. When anyone tried to cross it, that wicked Troll would swallow them whole!

The little Billy Goat Gruff stepped onto the bridge first. *Trippity-skip, trippity-skip* went his feet across the wobbly boards.

"Who's that tripping and skipping over my bridge?" roared the Troll.

The little Billy Goat Gruff shivered and shook. "It's just me, the little Billy Goat Gruff," he squeaked. "I'm going to the hillside to graze on the grass."

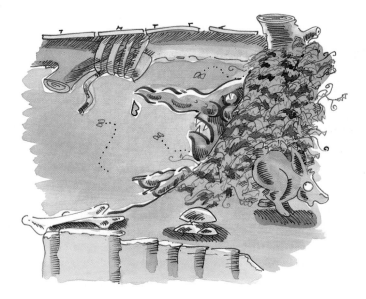

"Oh, no, you're not," roared the Troll, "because I am going to eat you up!"

"Not me, I'm too small! I won't do at all," said the little Billy Goat Gruff. "Wait for my middle brother. As you'll soon see, he's bigger than me."

The Troll smacked his lips. "Hurry up then. Get on your way!" he bellowed.

The little Billy Goat Gruff skipped the rest of the way across the bridge as quickly as his feet could carry him.

Not long afterwards, the middle Billy Goat Gruff stepped onto the bridge. *Trampity-stamp, trampity-stamp* went his feet across the wobbly boards.

"Who's that tramping and stamping over my bridge?" roared the Troll.

The middle Billy Goat Gruff quivered and quaked. "It's just me, the middle Billy Goat Gruff," he bleated. "I'm going to the hillside to graze on the grass."

"Oh, no, you're not," shouted the Troll, "because I am going to eat you up!"

"Not me, I'm too small! I won't do at all," said the middle Billy Goat Gruff. "Wait for my older brother. As you'll soon see, he's bigger than me."

The Troll smacked his lips and rubbed his great fat belly. "Hurry up then. Get on your way!" he roared.

The middle Billy Goat Gruff stamped the rest of the way across the bridge as fast as his feet could carry him.

A short time later, the big Billy Goat Gruff stepped onto the bridge. *Clompity-stomp, clompity-stomp* went his feet across the wobbly boards.

"Who's that clomping and stomping over my bridge?" roared the Troll.

The big Billy Goat Gruff didn't shiver and shake. He didn't quiver and quake. He stood straight and tall with his horns held high. "It's me, the big Billy Goat Gruff," he boomed. "I'm going to the hillside to graze on the grass."

"Oh, no, you're not," shouted the Troll, "because I am going to eat you up!"

"Come and get me then," said the big Billy Goat Gruff. "My hoofs and horns will be the end of you, and my brothers and I will dine on Troll stew."

The wicked Troll rushed up onto the bridge, thinking only of a billy-goat dinner. But the big Billy Goat Gruff was ready for him. He lowered his horns and charged.

*Clompity-stomp, clompity-stomp* went his heavy feet as he thundered toward the Troll.

*Bang!* The big Billy Goat Gruff knocked the Troll over the side of the bridge and down into the cold dark river. From that day to this, no one has heard so much as a whisper from that wicked old Troll.

The three Billy Goats Gruff never did dine on Troll stew. Now they cross the bridge whenever they want to graze on the clover and grass and wild berries high on the hillside. They eat from morning till night, growing a whole lot fuller and a little bit fatter every day.

# The Three Little Pigs

Once a Mother Pig said to her three little Piglets, "It's time for you to go out into the world and set up homes of your own." As she kissed each one good-bye she said, "Remember, my sweet Piglet, watch out for the big bad Wolf!"

Off went the three little Pigs to seek their fortunes. The first took the high road, the second took the low road and the third took the middle road.

The first little Pig hadn't gone far when he met a man carrying a huge bale of straw.

"Please, sir, may I have some of that straw to build a house?" asked the little Pig.

"Indeed you may," said the man and he gave him a big bundle.

The little Pig piled the straw this way and that way, and he ended up with a shaky straw house. Just as he was settling in, along came the big bad Wolf.

"Little Pig, little Pig, let me come in," called the Wolf.

"Not by the hair on my chinny-chin-chin!" cried the little Pig.

"Then I'll huff and I'll puff and I'll blow your house in!" growled the Wolf. With a huff and a puff he blew the shaky straw house to shreds. And — *gobble, gobble, gulp, gulp* — he swallowed the first little Pig.

The second little Pig walked along the low road until he met a man pushing a cart stacked high with sticks.

"Please, sir, may I have some of those sticks to build a house?" asked the little Pig.

"Indeed you may," said the man and he gave him a large stack.

The little Pig piled the sticks this way and that way, and he ended up with a very rickety stick house. Soon after he moved in, along came the big bad Wolf.

"Little Pig, little Pig, let me come in," called the Wolf.

"Not by the hair on my chinny-chin-chin!" cried the little Pig.

"Then I'll huff and I'll puff and I'll blow your house in!" growled the Wolf. With a huff and a puff he blew the rickety stick house to pieces. And — *gobble, gobble, gulp, gulp* — he swallowed the second little Pig.

The third little Pig followed the middle road until he met a man pulling a great wagonload of bricks.

"Please, sir, may I have some of those bricks to build myself a house?" asked the little Pig.

"Indeed you may," said the man and he gave him a generous pile.

The little Pig laid the bricks side by side. Then he piled them just so, one on top of the other. This little Pig ended up with a sturdy brick house. He was busy hanging curtains when along came the big bad Wolf.

"Little Pig, little Pig, let me come in," called the Wolf.

"Not by the hair on my chinny-chin-chin!" cried the little Pig.

"Then I'll huff and I'll puff and I'll blow your house in!" growled the Wolf. He huffed and he puffed. He huffed until his nose turned red. He puffed until his throat went dry. But no matter how hard he tried, he couldn't blow the sturdy brick house in.

"You'll never get me, you old blowhard!" laughed the little Pig.

The Wolf took a minute to catch his breath. Then he put a big wide smile on his face and said sweetly, "Dear little Pig, do you like turnips?"

"I certainly do," replied the little Pig.

"Then I'll call for you tomorrow morning at seven o'clock," said the Wolf. "I'll show you where to find the juiciest turnips in Farmer Flagg's field."

"I don't trust that Wolf one bit!" said the little Pig to himself, so he was up and away to Farmer Flagg's field at six o'clock the next morning. When the Wolf came by at seven, he smelled turnips cooking.

"You're too late," the little Pig called out. "I've already been to Farmer Flagg's and back."

The Wolf was angry, but he smiled and said, "Dear little Pig, do you like apples?"

"I certainly do," replied the little Pig.

"Then I'll call for you tomorrow morning at six o'clock," said the Wolf. "I'll show you where to find the ripest apples in Granny Grinny's orchard. We'll pick a basket together."

When the Wolf came by the next morning, the little Pig wasn't home. The Wolf quickly set off for Granny Grinny's. There he spotted the little Pig, high up in the apple tree, filling his basket.

"We were supposed to pick apples together," the Wolf called up to him in a growly voice.

"Here's your share," the little Pig called back. He took three plump apples from the basket and threw them as far as he could. "Catch them if you can!" he shouted.

While the Wolf chased after the apples, the little Pig scrambled out of the tree and ran home. When the Wolf came back, the little Pig was gone.

"Where did that little porker go?" growled the Wolf. Off he raced to the little Pig's house. He peeked in the window. There was the little Pig safe inside, peeling apples.

The Wolf was furious, but he smiled and said, "Dear little Pig, do you like fairs?"

"I certainly do," replied the little Pig.

"Then I'll call for you this afternoon at three o'clock," said the Wolf. "We'll go to Shanklin Fair together."

"I'll be ready for you," promised the little Pig.

"You won't fool me this time," muttered the Wolf. He arrived at the little Pig's house half-an-hour early. But once again the little Pig wasn't home. The Wolf set off to Shanklin Fair, dreaming of a fine pork-chop dinner.

Meanwhile, the little Pig had gone to the fair all by himself. He had seen everything there was to see, and was on his way home carrying the large butter churn he'd bought. As he came over the top of a high hill, the little Pig saw the Wolf at the bottom.

As quick as you can say *big bad Wolf*, the little Pig turned the butter churn on its side and jumped in. *Thumpity-bump, thumpity-bump*, down the hill he rolled. *Bumpity-thump, bumpity-thump*, he sent the Wolf flying so high into the sky that he was never seen again.

The third little Pig rolled all the way to his front door. Then he went inside and had a delicious dinner of boiled turnips and warm apple bread spread thickly with fresh creamy butter.